Also by Mark Binder

Autobiographical Fiction

Tall Tales, Whoppers and Lies
Dead at Knotty Oak
The Rationalization Diet

Folk Tales

The Bed Time Story Book
Classic Stories for Boys and Girls

The Chelm Series

The Council of Wise Women
Matzah Mishugas
The Brothers Schlemiel
A Hanukkah Present
A Chanukah Present (audio)
The World's Best Challah
The Brothers Schlemiel from Birth to Bar Mitzvah (audio)

Matzah Mishugas

Mark Binder

Mark Binder

Light Publications

Design by Beth Hellman
Design consultation by Heather Feiring and Claudia Summers

Thanks to all my readers and listeners, especially Jim Rosenberg, Vida Hellman, Ida and Steve Colchamiro, Rose Pavlov, Nava Levine and of course Harry, Francesca, Max, and Elaine K. Binder.
Thanks to the Rhode Island Bureau of Jewish Education.
Stories in this collection have appeared in: *Cricket Magazine, The Jewish Daily Forward, Washington Jewish Week, The Shofar, Being Jewish, The Observer, American Jewish World, The Jewish Chronicle, Jewish Western Bulletin, The Jewish Journal, Arizona Jewish Post, Greater Phoenix Jewish News, Chicago JUF News, Chicago Jewish Star, Charlotte Jewish News, American Jewish World, Jewish Free Press, The Chelmsford Independent, The Jewish Advocate & Jewish Times, Ohio Jewish Chronicle, The Wisconsin Jewish Chronicle, The School Magazine...*

ISBN 0-9824707-1-1
ISBN-13 978-0-9824707-1-8
Printed in the United States of America
10 9 8 7 6 5 4 3 2 1

Light Publications
PO Box 2462
Providence, RI 02906
U. S. A.
www.lightpublications.com

Have an excellent day!

For my family
all the Binders,
Brennans, Colchamiros, Aarons,
Hagens and Berlowe-Binders.

Next year, let's have another seder. . . .

Contents

Foreword

Welcome to Chelm! Welcome to the village of fools. Eighty households, a few dirt roads, more chickens than people, and a wealth of love, lore, misadventure and silliness. Once again we will rub elbows with Rabbi Kibbitz and Mrs. Chaipul, the Steins, Golds, Cohens and of course the Schlemiels.

People have asked me why I write these stories. After all, this is the third book in my Chelm series. And I have often wondered myself.

They began by mishap. I was editing a Jewish newspaper, and one day someone forgot to submit a crucial feature story. We were on deadline, and I wrote my first tale of Chelm.

At the time, I had not read the Chelm stories of I.B. Singer or Sholem Alechem. I did remember the slim collection of stories, more anecdotes and jokes, of catching the moon in a rain barrel and angels dropping dolts from the sky.

My Chelm is, I hope, different. While I enjoy the humor and misadventure (and schmaltz), I relish the individuality and strength of each character, and take joy in how they meet and mingle.

Somehow, Chelm has become a second home for me, where the name of Reb Cantor the Merchant can evoke an entire scenario. My Chelm books don't need to be read in any particular order, because many of the stories happen in parallel tracks. In "Home is Where the Seder Is," Abraham Schlemiel is grown and moved far away to America. In "Mrs. Chaipul's Lead Sinker Matzah Balls," the caterer and the rabbi are not yet married, but by "Seder Switch" they are firmly wedlocked.

Years pass and even the characters of fiction must change.

Was life in Chelm simpler? Perhaps. For me,

it is a joy to write of a time before computers and cell phones. All communication was face to face or by words on a page. If you missed a train, you couldn't text ahead. If you were lost, there was no GPS. And if you were hungry, you couldn't phone the supermarket for a delivery.

In short, the troubles you had were very real and inescapable.

In other works of fiction, such a time and place might seem lonely, but in Chelm, friends and family and community surround everyone.

These are not religious tales, by and large. You don't need to be Jewish to enjoy them. Although this collection is firmly set around the season, needs and requirements of Passover, the stories are about the people more than the practices, and their relationships more than the religion.

For me, Chelm is the source of my family and my community. It is the idealized place and time that we left behind and can never return to… except in story.

And if that makes me a fool, so be it. When I walk down the street and hear the strain of a violin, I don't really look for a Fiddler on the Roof, but I do smile and maybe dance a few steps.

Thank you for dancing with me.

– Mark Binder, *Pembroke Villa, Providence*

Mrs. Chaipul's Lead Sinker Matzah Balls

Mrs. Chaipul is a wonderful cook. When you run the only kosher restaurant in the village of Chelm, you have to be. Her *kugel* is incredible; her *kreplach* are tender and moist; her corned beef and cabbage melt in your mouth; her roasted potatoes are hot and crisp; and her split pea soup is so rich and robust, you'd swear it was *treif.* Even her potato latkes, which once were the scourge of Hanukkah, have improved greatly over the past few years—that is another story.

But her lead sinker matzah balls will never change. This is the story of those matzah balls—and how they saved Chelm.

When Mrs. Chaipul first moved to Chelm, she brought her matzah ball recipe with her. It had been in her family for generations, passed down in secret from mother to daughter.

In the Chaipul family, jaw-breaking matzah balls were an immutable tradition, like plucking a chicken on the first day of spring. Every year, the Chaipul men joked that the secret was building construction mortar—a comment that was met with stony silence by the women. At one Seder, Mrs. Chaipul's grandfather Moishe argued for six hours that if the pyramids had only been built from his wife's matzah balls, then they would still be standing. Never mind the fact that his son-in-law, Sam Klammerdinger (Mrs. Chaipul's first husband, may he rest in peace), tried to convince Moishe that the pyramids really were still standing. It was indisputable that, undigested, a Chaipul Knaidel could last for generations.

In Chelm, the villagers' first taste of the Chaipul Knaidel was the second year after she had opened the restaurant. The first year, Mrs. Chaipul was too busy to clean and make the facility kosher for Passover, so she shut down and arranged for a *goyishe* intermediary to buy the restaurant for the eight-day festival.

During that first Passover in Chelm, Mrs. Chaipul was invited to eat at the house of every villager. After all, with her shop closed, someone had to feed her.

Naturally she accepted Shoshana Cantor's invitation. Who wouldn't? Wasn't Reb Cantor the merchant the wealthiest man in Chelm? Wouldn't his Passover feast be the most sumptuous?

And it was. Mrs. Chaipul arrived well before sunset to find that all the work in the kitchen was done. Shoshana had servants to help her! When the table was set, it was beautiful. There were seven forks, three knives, and fourteen spoons. Mrs. Chaipul was at a loss to know where to begin. What did you do with seven forks except put them on the table, wash them and then put them back in the drawer?

Still, the *charoses* was tasty, with a hint of fresh orange from the Holy Land, and the matzah was

Reb Stein the baker's finest *shmura*, round and crisp.

Then came the chicken soup, and for Mrs. Chaipul this was both a shock and a revelation. She looked at the walnut-sized matzah balls floating in the soup, and this in itself gave her pause. Floating matzah balls? She had never seen such a thing! She sighed, exercised her jaw a bit, lifted a knaidel with her spoon, and bit.

When you're expecting to bite a rock and instead your teeth sink into lightly whipped air, it comes as something of a surprise. Her jaw dropped open as the matzah ball melted in her mouth. She sat there with the spoon held suspended in mid-air for quite some time.

"Is everything all right?" Shoshana Cantor asked. "Is there enough salt?"

Mrs. Chaipul realized that she was being rude, and she quickly closed her mouth. Her teeth cut through the matzah ball like a hot knife through butter. She chewed, and in seconds the matzah ball had dissolved as if it had never been.

"Interesting," she said quietly. And then she added, so as not to offend her hostess, "Quite tasty."

It was the same at every house she visited in Chelm. Far from being the stones of affliction, the matzah balls were soft, chewy, and, above all, edible.

By the end of Passover, Mrs. Chaipul was disheartened and confused. Had her family been doing something wrong for so many years? Or were the villagers of Chelm the misguided ones?

She took her concerns to Rabbi Kibbitz. This was in the days before they were married. In fact, it was one of the first private conferences that she and the learned man had. She explained her problem and waited for pearls of wisdom.

He was no help at all. "*Kabalah* I know," he said. "But cooking?" He shrugged. "I eat what's in front of me. Too much, if you ask some of the villagers." Then he laughed and patted his great stomach.

Mrs. Chaipul set the questions aside and went back to her restaurant.

A year passed as if it was an instant, and once again Passover was fast approaching.

This year Mrs. Chaipul was determined to be open for business, if not for the Seders, then for every other meal. She knew that most housewives only knew how to prepare matzah so many ways.

She had in her possession the *Chaipul Pesach Cookbook*, which detailed more than fourteen hundred recipes made with matzah meal and potato starch alone and in combination.

Once again she ate her Seder at the Cantor house and once again she was polite. This time, however, it was Reb Cantor who noticed her face.

"I understand that your restaurant will be open for Passover this year," he said. "Will you be making matzah ball soup?"

Mrs. Chaipul grinned. "Yes, of course. It wouldn't be Passover without the famous Chaipul Knaidel. I missed them last year and I thought that I would give them away this year to make up for my mistake."

Reb Cantor's eyes widened. "You're giving away free food in a village of Jews?"

"Well," said Mrs. Chaipul with a shrug, "The matzah balls will be free, but the soup will still cost."

Reb Cantor smiled with understanding.

On the second day of Passover, despite the fact that it was pouring down rain, the line for Mrs. Chaipul's restaurant snaked out the door. She sent her customers home, wading back and forth through the muddy streets, to bring their kosher-for-Passover soup bowls so she wouldn't have to spend the whole day and night washing dishes. Fortunately, she had anticipated the crowd, so she had made six kettles the size of washtubs full of matzah balls. Even so, she still wasn't sure there was going to be enough, so she had to set a limit of one per customer—at least until everyone had firsts.

She ladled soup and a knaidel into each bowl and said with a smile, "Remember that we were once slaves in Egypt."

The villagers thought this was quaint enough, although they were puzzled when the matzah ball sank to the bottom of the bowl with a clank.

Then they looked for a place to sit. The counters were full; the tables were packed. Many young men and women were forced to slurp standing up.

The restaurant was crowded elbow to elbow, tighter than the shul for *erev Kol Nidre*. Still the villagers felt jolly. Outside it was cold and wet and bucketing down rain. In Mrs. Chaipul's restaurant they were all warm and cozy, glowing with anticipation.

The soup was sweet and savory, rich with the snap of parsnip and perfectly peeled slices of carrot. It was, in the words of Rabbi Kibbitz, "Good enough to cure even an uncommon cold."

And then it was time to eat the matzah balls.

They were bigger than those the villagers had been accustomed to. Instead of the size of walnuts or chicken eggs, Mrs. Chaipul's matzah balls were as big as ripe apples. It wasn't so easy to get such a large knaidel into your mouth or even onto your spoon. They were so heavy that one child was forced to balance his bowl on his knees and use two hands to lift his.

At last came the bite, that first bite, the one that defines a matzah ball—and the matzah ball cook—forever.

Ow! It hurt. It wasn't so much hard like a rock, but it certainly was dense, like a clay brick before it has set in its mold. Your teeth could get into it, but it was hard work, like sawing wood with a nail file. After two minutes the villagers began to have second thoughts but found that their teeth had sunk in so deeply that they were trapped and there was no choice but to go on. After five minutes their jaws began to ache, and the villagers started to wonder whether Mrs. Chaipul's family had all died of lockjaw and starvation.

At last, one by one the villagers bit through with a sudden snap of tooth against tooth and were struck by the realization that they still had to chew the whole bite up because it would be messy and rude to spit it out onto the floor.

So chew they did. The afternoon dragged into evening, the rain was still pouring, and still they were chewing.

The flavor was phenomenally *goob* and robust, but it went on and on and on. Everyone nodded and smiled. And then they chewed some more.

It was starting to get dark when, all of a sudden young Doodle, the village orphan, burst into the restaurant. He had forgotten that there was free food and had been wandering through the village looking for someone to tell his news.

"Mrs. Chaipul! Rabbi Kibbitz! The dam on the Bug River has burst! A flood is coming."

There wasn't time to think or plan. The villagers stampeded out of the restaurant, and ran to the banks of the river where the dam they built years ago had finally broken.

A wall of water was rushing toward them. In minutes, it looked like the village of Chelm would be washed away and drowned, forgotten like the village that Noah, from the safety of his ark, had watched vanish.

No one could speak—partly because they were in shock and partly because they were all still chewing. The villagers were so upset, they hadn't even bothered to put down their bowls and spoons.

Mrs. Chaipul, who had been too busy serving to eat a bite, broke the silence with a command.

"Throw your matzah balls into the river," she shouted. "Aim upstream from the break in the dam!"

The villagers did as they were told. Matzah balls went flying. They were caught by the current and forced into the crack where they became lodged and stuck fast. More and more matzah balls flew into the river, landing with loud sploshes until the gap in the dam was sealed tight and not even a dribble leaked through.

The villagers wanted to sigh, but first they had to swallow, which they did, just as the rain stopped and the setting sun emerged from behind a cloud.

And then they cheered: "Mazel Tov for Mrs. Chaipul's Famous Knaidels!"

Mrs. Chaipul beamed and *kvelled*.

Then, much to her surprise, Rabbi Kibbitz kissed her on the cheek and whispered into her ear, "Delicious. You should never change that recipe."

What could she do? She didn't.

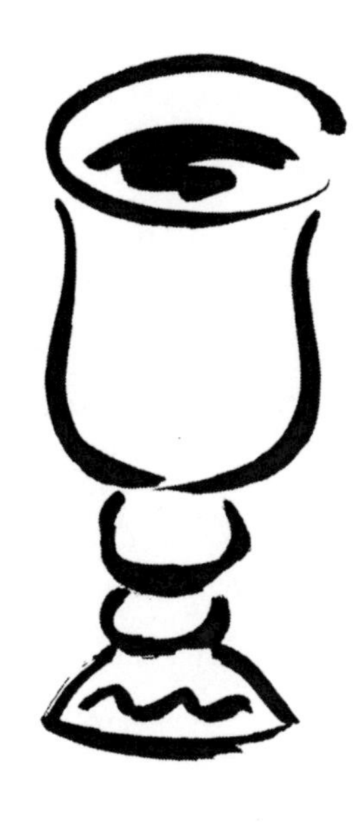

Seder Switch

"Do you know what I dreamed about last night?" Mrs. Chaipul asked her unsuspecting husband.

The chief rabbi of Chelm shook his head. "Hmm?" he asked, not yet fully awake.

"I was leading the Passover Seder," she said.

The rabbi blinked. "You were what? You were leading the Seder?"

"And what's so wrong with that?" Chanah Chaipul said. "When my first husband, Sam

Klammerdinger, rest his soul, lost the power of speech, I led the Seder. Who else was going to do it?"

The rabbi sputtered, coughed, opened his mouth, and then closed it. He had married late in life, but after the incident of the lethal latkes had been quick to learn the first rule, "Never say anything you might regret later—no matter how right you may think you are."

"You look awful," his wife said. "Perhaps you should come into the restaurant for some chicken soup."

"Perhaps I will," the rabbi said. Or perhaps, he thought, I'll just go back to bed.

The rabbi had a suspicious feeling that trouble was brewing. When they were first married, Chanah had caused quite a stir when she had refused to close her restaurant or take his name. Since then, everyone in the village of Chelm assumed that she was the ruler of their house. And, if pressed, the rabbi himself might admit that held some truth.

What would they say if Chanah got it into her head to lead the Passover Seder?

Rabbi Kibbitz shuddered and tugged on his beard.

By noon the delegation appeared in the door of the Rabbi's study.

"Have you heard this nonsense?" said Reb Gold.

"It's in the Torah!" said Reb Cantor.

"I don't believe it," said Reb Kimmelman. "I traveled the world from Chelm to Palestine, and not once until today have I heard such a thing."

Then all spoke at once, and Rabbi Kibbitz understood not a word. At last he calmed them down, and appointed Reb Cantor to give him the news.

"The women all want to lead the Seder this year," Reb Cantor said. "Can they do that?"

"Never mind can they do that," interrupted Reb Gold, "should they even think such a thing?"

"It's nonsense," Reb Kimmelman added. "Pure and simple."

Rabbi Kibbitz chose his next words carefully. "Why is it nonsense? True, it is traditional for the men to lead the Seder, but I have spent the morning in study and have found no law prohibiting women from taking over the role."

The crowded study was silent.

"But," said the rabbi at last, "I have an idea. If they want to lead the Seder, then it is only right that we should prepare the meal."

This suggestion produced shouts of outrage. In Chelm, and throughout the world, women cooked and men worked. That was the order of things.

"Relax." Rabbi Kibbitz raised his hands to calm the assembly. "Our wives will never agree to let us take over their kitchens. Just as we feel that leading the Seder is a man's job, they also feel that making the dinner is a woman's job. How could it be otherwise?"

Ahhh! A collective sigh of relief rippled through the room. As a group, the men thanked the Rabbi, and hurried home to tell their wives the bargain.

Needless to say, once again, Rabbi Kibbitz was completely wrong.

One after another, the housewives of Chelm (even Mrs. Chaipul) jumped at the opportunity to lead the Seder. They also unanimously agreed that, if the women were to lead, it was only fitting that the men put on the aprons and stir the soup.

"But," every man said to his beloved, "I don't know how to cook!"

"Neither do I know how to lead the Seder," answered the women, "but that will not stop me."

For the next few weeks, not one man in Chelm had a kind word to say about their learned rabbi. On the streets they passed him with respectful silence. In shul they performed their duties and left quickly instead of staying afterwards for a chat with tea.

At last, Rabbi Kibbitz got down on his knees and prayed aloud to the Almighty for assistance. But, as it had been from the time of the prophets, the King of Kings kept his silence.

So, Rabbi Kibbitz did what any man resigned to his situation does—he made the best of it. He searched through the shul's library until he found the cookbooks that his grandmother had donated, and he began making notes of recipes. Soon he was joined by one after another of the husbands, as well of some of their eldest sons.

Ordinary work in Chelm dragged to a halt as one by one the men began to prepare for this greatest of Jewish feasts. They went to the market to find the best chickens. They bought their matzah from the baker's wife, because the baker was busy chopping onions. Each worked on a dessert that they remembered from childhood, and they traded samples. They got together in a group and made a huge communal batch of chopped liver, which actually tasted pretty good. Their spirits began rise.

At the same time, doubts began to form in the minds of the women. What if they did something wrong during the Seder? There was so much to remember. Did you stand up while washing your hands, or sit? Should the bitter herbs be passed to the right, or to the left?

But the greatest fear that the women had was similar to the men's—"What if he cooks a better meal than me?"

At last, erev Pesach arrived. The streets of Chelm grew quiet as every family gathered in a topsy-turvy home.

Tonight, the husbands lit the candles and the wives said the blessing over the matzah. Tonight the wives asked the four questions while the husbands scurried into the kitchen to check on the soup. The husbands giggled when the wives made a mistake. The wives drank all four cups of wine, while the husbands had time only to sip theirs.

And at last, when the evening was done, and the Seders finished, and the dishes cleared, every man, woman and child of Chelm fell into a completely exhausted sleep.

The next day, all awoke feeling mysteriously rested. As if they all shared the same thought, they gathered in the village synagogue, which was soon as full as on the holiest of holy days.

The room quieted as Rabbi Kibbitz mounted the *bimah*. He smiled at his people and said simply, "I think we all appreciate Pesach just a little more."

Seders in Chelm were never quite the same. The communal liver chopping, for example, became something of an annual event. Most families returned to their old habits, but others, like the Kibbitz-Chaipul household, found a happy compromise.

From that Pesach on, the Rebbe and Rebbitzen together shared in the leading and in the cooking.

For, as Rabbi Kibbitz liked to say while he helped his bride wash her hands, is not the contribution of every person precious?

The Mega-Matzah

Once, in the village of Chelm, a disaster struck right in the middle of the Passover Seder. There was chaos, food flew through the air, children ran shrieking to their mothers. It was *mishugas*, and…

But wait, it is important that you understand a few details.

Every year, weather permitting, (which in Chelm was not very often,) all the villagers gathered in the round square outside the synagogue to celebrate a communal Pesach feast. It was a potluck affair, with each family of Chelm contributing some portion of the meal.

Rabbi Kibbitz supplied the blessings. Mrs. Chaipul would bring her famous lead-ball knaidlach soup. Reb Cantor prepared gallons of kosher l'Pesach homemade wine, and poured hundreds of cups, four per person (with kosher grape juice for the youngsters). The Levitzkys, Reb and Mrs., worked together and dazzled everyone's sweet tooth with their mysterious chopped apple Sephardic charoset.

And, every year, the baker, Reb Stein, baked matzah for all of Chelm, with the aid of his friend, Rabbi Yohon Abrahms, the schoolteacher.

This particular year, however, Reb Stein had decided that he would create the world's largest matzah.

Now, in the past, one of the czars, Fyodor, The Not So Great, had commissioned, from the bakers in Moscow, an unleavened bread the size of a tabletop. Jews in London had once witnessed a *hamotzi* over a matzah as big as a horse cart. And it was rumored that in Jerusalem bakers had been developing for centuries a secret recipe that they claimed would permit them to rebuild the

Holy Temple completely out of matzah within a week, if the Messiah should ever come and call for it.

Given such stiff competition, Rabbi Yohon Abrahms argued that Reb Stein could never hope to compete.

"Chelm is a small village," Rabbi Abrahms said, "what do we need with something so big? Be careful that you don't call down the wrath of the Almighty for your arrogance."

"Phooey," said Reb Stein. "I will be written into the *Gibberish Book of World Records*, alongside the man with the largest inflamed toe."

Before entering his chametz-free workshop, with its huge brick oven, Reb Stein would wash, change his clothes, and put on gloves and a veil, like a bride, to prevent contamination. For weeks, he slaved, "Like our forefathers in Egypt," he claimed. His eyes took on a burning look, or perhaps it was just the singes on his eyebrows from the intense heat.

There were hundreds of rejects, broken scraps of matzah that looked like blackened shingles, and tasted like unsalted tree bark.

So, on the day before Pesach, with none of their individual matzah orders filled yet, the citizens were both curious, and concerned about the progress of their baker.

"I hear", said Reb Gold, "that if he fails, he'll shoot himself."

"That would be bad," said Joseph Katz, "because he still owes me money from our *Chanukah dreidel* game."

"You'd better talk with him now," said Reb Gold. "The man is close to madness."

But just then, Joel Cantor, Reb Cantor's youngest son, ran up to his father, and breathlessly announced, "Reb Stein has made the biggest matzah in the world!"

"Well, good," interrupted Joseph Katz, "I'll still make sure I collect after the Seder."

Then, from around the corner came Reb Stein, dressed elegantly in white, with a team of four horses struggling to pull three wagons lashed together!

Everyone craned their necks for a look, but the Mega-Matzah was hidden from sight by a huge matzah cover made from fourteen bed sheets borrowed, after a ferocious argument, from Mrs. Stein's linen closet.

"Tomorrow night!" Reb Stein laughed, as he rode his wagons into the round village square. "Tomorrow night, you will all see, and admire!"

"He sounds sick," said Reb Gold.

"He needs help," agreed Reb Cantor.

All through the Seder, the citizens stared at the Mega Matzah's cover.

It was so gigantic! It had been moved off the wagons, and now four whole banquet tables were devoted to supporting it. The men who had moved it from the wagons to the tables said that it weighed more than all of Mrs. Chaipul's cast-iron knaidels put together! (And that was something!)

After the four questions, and following the *hamotzi*, Rabbi Kibbitz turned to Reb Stein, who nodded to Rabbi Yohon Abrahms.

"Not yet!" said Reb Stein. "I made a special, smaller matzah. To keep the suspense."

It was a good thing, too, the poor baker thought. The man from the *Gibberish Book of World Records* was late. Reb Stein was nervous, and kept looking over his shoulder. His creation needed to be witnessed and documented!

Helpfully, Rabbi Yohon Abrahms giggled as he peeked under the matzah covers and brought out a matzah that was the size of a window!

The Mini-Mega-Matzah was not gargantuan, but it tasted fine.

With the help of more than four cups of Reb Cantor's wine, the villagers finally managed to choke down Mrs. Chaipul's shot putt knaidel's, and thoroughly enjoyed the rest of the huge feast and service!

Then it was time for dessert—the largest Afikomen known to mankind—the Mega-Matzah!

Reb Stein rose from his seat of honor, and scanned the village's round square for any sign of the record-keeper from the *Gibberish Book*. If the man didn't show up soon, his hopes would be dashed and masterpiece would be devoured.

Fortunately for Reb Stein's ulcer, a horse carriage pulled into the small village, drove past the Yeshiva, and stopped at the edge of the feast. An old man peered out from the carriage's window at the four covered tables.

Reb Stein grinned, grasped the matzah cover, and with a grand flourish (tugging several times because Mrs. Stein's sheets were so heavy) unveiled his masterpiece.

Which was when the *mishugas* that was mentioned at the beginning of this story began…

There was chaos, leftover food flew through the air, and children ran shrieking to their mothers. As one person, the villagers of Chelm gasped.

Because, instead of a matzah instead of a giant cracker, instead of a humungous piece of unleavened bread, what the people of Chelm saw before them was a large… a flat… a black… piece of roof. (Yes, roof, with shingles and all.)

Reb Stein, his ulcer forgotten, clutched at his heart. The man from *Gibberish* shook his head sadly, and pulling the drapes of his horse carriage shut ordered his horse driver to leave.

You wouldn't have thought that such disappointment would cause anyone amusement, but just then, Rabbi Yohon Abrahms and ten of his Yeshiva students fell out of their chairs with laughter!

In the dead of night, Rabbi Abrahms explained between guffaws, he and his students had switched the Mega-Matzah with the roof from the Yeshiva science laboratory. And now, the matzah was on the roof, and the roof was on the matzah tables.

All the citizens of Chelm ran to the school. The horse carriage from *Gibberish* was just ahead of them, about to leave Chelm forever.

Reb Stein gasped as he saw his masterpiece of white and brown, perfectly baked unleavened bread suspended high on the walls of the place of learning. He jumped up and down for the man in the cart to come back, and shouted, "Wait! Wait! Look at the size of it!"

But by then the cart was long gone, and with it went Reb Stein's chance at record-making history.

After not so long, some impatient children suggested that it was still time for dessert, so Rabbi Abrahms and his Yeshiva students, with their backs straining, took the Mega-Matzah off the roof and returned it to the Seder.

The Afikomen was broken up into large plate-sized pieces, and eaten with appetites whetted by laughter. It was even more delicious than the first. Everyone said, "What a wonderful thing Reb Stein has done!"

(Not to mention that, when the meal was concluded, there was more than enough unleavened bread left to feed the entire village for the whole week of Pesach.)

Reb Stein, though he still makes the best matzah in the world, has never quite recovered. From that day to this, year-round, every cake, *challah*, biscuit and bread that he makes for his friend Rabbi Abrahms is as flat as a latke.

Rabbi Abrahms doesn't complain, though; he trusts that some day, with the help of the Almighty, he'll get another rise out of Reb Stein.

To Rise or Not to Rise

There was trouble in the small village of Chelm…

"I'm not going to school," said young David Gold, the cobbler's son. "God has commanded me to stay in bed."

"How can you say such a thing?" said his mother, Esther. She was quite tired from preparing and cleaning up the Passover Seder, and had been looking forward to a relaxing day in an empty house.

"It's Passover," David said, "and nothing is allowed to rise on Passover."

Esther Gold blinked at her son. "I don't think the Ruler of the Universe quite meant..."

"If I rise," said David, "I'll be breaking a commandment. You wouldn't want me to do that."

"No," Esther said. "I'm going to ask your father."

Esther left David and went downstairs to her husband's shop.

"Hello," said Joshua Gold. "Is it lunch time already?"

"David isn't going to school."

"Is he sick?"

Esther shook her head and explained.

"What a thing," said the father.

"I know," said the mother.

"We'd better ask the rabbi."

Off they went to Mrs. Chaipul's restaurant where Rabbi Kibbitz had his morning coffee. After greetings and hellos, the Golds explained their problem.

"What a thing," said Mrs. Chaipul.

"That's what I said," said Reb Gold.

"But he's got a point," said Rabbi Kibbitz. "Bread is not allowed to rise during Passover."

"Nor cake," said Mrs. Chaipul.

"No bagels," said Reb Cantor, the merchant, who felt that matzah brie was a poor substitute for his bagel and shmear.

"But it's ridiculous," said Esther Gold. "If we can't rise in the morning, how will anything get done?"

"I don't know," said Rabbi Kibbitz, stroking his beard. "I just don't know..."

Word spread through Chelm like the parting of the Red Sea. On one side were the early risers, and on the other were the slugabeds.

The early risers were, of course, already up. They had things to do, places to go, people to see. For them, getting up early was a great joy and blessing.

The slugabeds also rejoiced at the news. Those who were already up, immediately hopped back into bed. For them, nothing was so sweet as a nap—morning, noon, afternoon, or evening, not to mention the night's slumber.

For three days, Chelm was a changed village.

At first, the early risers luxuriated in their newfound freedom from interruption by sleep.

"I am getting so much more done," Esther Gold said, as she whitewashed the kitchen at midnight by candlelight.

Simultaneously, the slugabeds, cozy and snug, relished their unlimited rest and relaxation. The sheets were warm, the pillows soft, and their dreams were sweet.

By the fourth morning, though…

The early risers were exhausted. In order not to break the commandment, they slept standing up, or leaning against a wall. Their blankets slipped off, and their pillows fell to the floor. It was not particularly restful, and all of their chores were done.

The slugabeds had problems of their own. Never mind that they had to crawl back and forth to the bathroom, or that they were forced to eat their meals on the dining room floor. It is quite difficult to drink from a glass while you're lying on your back or stomach. (This was in the days before straws.) Worst of all, they were not tired any more. Men, women and children who for years had complained about never getting enough rest were suddenly all slept out.

A meeting was called in Rabbi Kibbitz's bedroom where the Rabbi lay beneath his covers, impatient but wide awake.

Around the bed, stood Esther Gold, Reb Cantor the merchant, and Rabbi Yohon Abrahms, the Masghiach and head of the Yeshiva.

"This can't continue," said Esther Gold, blinking her eyes furiously to stay awake.

"A commandment's a commandment," Rabbi Yohon Abrahms said.

"There's got to be a solution," yawned Reb Cantor.

"I've been awake thinking," said Rabbi Kibbitz. "I have an idea."

"Go on," said Reb Cantor.

"Tell us," said Esther Gold.

Rabbi Kibbitz said, "What if we just get up?"

"I'm not sure I follow," said Reb Cantor, who had dozed off.

"If we get up, aren't we rising?" asked Rabbi Yohon Abrahms.

Wise Rabbi Kibbitz shrugged. "When we breathe, does not our chest rise and fall? And yet God did not command us to stop breathing. When bread rises, it does nothing else but rise.

When people get up, yes they rise. But we do other things."

"I'm not so sure," said Rabbi Yohon Abrahms.

At just that moment, Mrs. Chaipul, who had been eavesdropping at the door, burst into the Rabbi's bedroom banging a wooden spoon against a pot.

"Get up! Get up!" she yelled, banging loudly.

"Ahh!" Rabbi Kibbitz shouted. And he immediately jumped out of bed. "You see!"

In a matter of minutes, every early riser in Chelm was beating on a pot or a pan, and slugabeds throughout the village were leaping to their feet.

There was a great cheer as the divided village was briefly reunited.

However, a few moments later, the early risers were all in their beds, while the slugabeds, up and awake at last, went about their business.

"This is a fine state of affairs," said Joshua Gold to his son, David. "Your mother is fast asleep. What should we do?"

The boy, who had started the trouble in the first place, smiled at his father, and said, innocently, "Let's take a nap!"

The father laughed, but shook his head. "No."

And together they went fishing.

After that, all would have been back to normal in Chelm… except for the unusual fish that David Gold caught.

But that is another story.

Knock Knock

About that evening I went missing, it isn't much of a story. The night was pitch black and I became completely lost. Fortunately, I found myself at the door to a small house. They must not have received many strangers in those parts, because every one in the village was soon jammed into that tiny room. I spun a yarn about a boy named Tom Sawyer and a dead cat, which they quite appreciated. Comedy, I suppose, being universal. The next day I managed to find my way back to my tour. Good soup with odd dumplings.

—From a letter by Samuel Clemens to Elisha Bliss, American Publishing Company, 1868.

The Seder was well under way at the home of Martin and Chaya Levitsky in the small village of Chelm. Dinner was long finished, it was time to open the door for Elijah the Prophet, and Reb Levitsky asked for volunteers.

Since their children were grown and had gone off to seek their fortune, it was the Levitsky's custom to invite their neighbors Joshua Gold, the cobbler, his wife Esther, and their son David, as well as young Doodle, the village orphan to share their Pesach feast.

David nudged Doodle, and Doodle nudged David. Both giggled. It was far past their bedtime, but neither would admit to being tired.

Reb Levitsky put on a stern face. "Someone must go. It would not do for the Messiah's herald to wait outside in the cold, and be forced to knock."

Just then there was a loud knocking at the door.

Everyone in the room jumped!

"What was that?" whispered Doodle.

"Maybe it's Elijah," David teased.

"Hush," warned Esther Gold. "Do not make such jokes."

All were quite quiet, listening.

"Just the wind," said Reb Gold. "You need to fix those window shutters, Martin."

"We don't have any shutters," said Reb Levitsky. "Perhaps we should open the door."

"I'm not going," said Doodle. "I'm afraid of Elijah."

"Pish," said Chaya Levitsky, who was thinking about all the plates of food that needed to be soaked and cleaned before bed.

"Come," said Esther Gold, rising up. She extended her hands to the boys. "All three of us will go and open the door for Elijah."

"Wonderful," said Reb Levitsky. He raised Elijah's cup, and began whispering a blessing.

The two boys followed Mrs. Gold to the door. "Now," she said, "one of you must open it."

Doodle shook his head, and David shook his.

"You do it," said one.

"No, you," said the other.

"Both of you," compromised Mrs. Gold, with a look toward heaven asking the almighty for patience.

Both boys crept to the door, put their hands on the knob, turned and pulled.

"You see," said Mrs. Gold, but her calm reassurance evaporated the instant she saw the man standing in the doorway with his hand raised about to knock. "Eeep," she said instead.

He was a tall man, a stranger in a long dark coat. His hair was white, he had no beard, and his bushy mustache drooped down around both sides of his mouth.

"It's Elijah!" shouted young David, running back into the dining room.

"Aaaah!" shrieked Doodle, chasing after him.

Mrs. Gold, for her part, blinked twice more, and then collapsed into unconsciousness.

"Maybe he's Lebanese," said Reb Stein's voice.

Mrs. Gold's eyes fluttered open. She found herself sitting upright in a chair in the Levitsky's dining room, which was now crowded with nearly two dozen of Chelm's most prominent citizens.

"No," said Reb Kimmelman, who had traveled to the Holy Land and back. "That's not Lebanese."

Chaya Levitsky passed Esther Gold a glass of hot tea.

The stranger was sitting at the table, finishing of a bowl of matzah ball soup, as if he was starved.

"Well," said Rabbi Kibbitz, "He doesn't speak Hebrew, Yiddish, Russian or Polish. What else is there?"

Just then the visitor, who did not seem at all flustered by the attention, made a gesture that caused everyone in the room to gasp. He pretended to hold something in his hands, and then he pretended to break it apart and wipe the broken pieces inside his soup bowl.

"He wants bread?" said Reb Cohen. "To sop up his soup?"

"Shouldn't Elijah know it's Pesach?" whispered Mrs. Chaipul.

"Nonsense," said Rabbi Kibbitz. "He is telling us that his broken heart has been mended by the healing power of the chicken soup."

"Ahhh," said everyone, nodding happily while Mrs. Levitsky kvelled with pleasure.

"If he's Elijah," said young Doodle, "does that mean that the end of the world is near?"

"Hush," said Reb Levitsky. "Why don't you go upstairs to bed?"

"No, no," calmed Rabbi Kibbitz. "The child is asking a valid question. If it is the creator's will, Elijah will tell us in his good time."

As if he understood the Rabbi's words, the stranger pushed his plate away, mopped his face with a napkin, cleared his throat and stood.

Then he spoke. He talked for hours and hours. His eyes were bright, his hands animated, and his words were rich and filled with meaning.

The villagers of Chelm sat shoulder to shoulder in the crowded dining room, listening transfixed. The candles burned low, but still they could not look away.

Not one of them, of course, understood a single word.

Two hours later, maybe three, his voice had not faltered, but eventually it slowed and his tone lowered and quieted until the room was, at last, silent.

Still no one moved. The candles flickered. The stranger's eyes flitted around the room, expectantly. "Well?" he seemed to say. "Well?"

What could one say? The women and men of Chelm were known throughout the countryside as wise people. They glanced from one to another.

Even Rabbi Kibbitz, the wisest of all seemed at a loss.

And then Little Doodle, who had fallen asleep on Chaya Levitsky's lap, suddenly snored—incredibly loudly for such a small boy.

"SNnHonnnk!"

The stranger's face looked utterly serious for a moment longer, and his shoulders began to shudder and shake.

All of the Chelmites gasped, wondering if they were about to witness the wrath of Elijah.

Then the stranger's odd beardless face shattered into a grin, and he began laughing loudly.

Soon, the whole house was filled with the deafening roar of laughter, which itself dissolved into the joyous songs that fill the close of every Seder. Even the stranger joined in, singing along in his foreign tongue.

The next morning the visitor was gone before anyone else awoke, and he has not yet returned.

Still, a tradition was born. If you ever see someone dozing off in classes at school, at speeches by politicians, at operas or even in Shul when the hour grows late and the sermon goes on, don't be in such a hurry to wake them. They are simply celebrating Elijah's visit to the small village of Chelm.

As it is said in Chelm, "To hear is human, to snore divine."

The Last Temptation of Rabbi Kibbitz

It was the seventh day of Passover, and Rabbi Kibbitz was proud that he hadn't had a thought of *chometz* in days. It was the first time in his life that he hadn't spent every waking hour obsessing about all the foods he couldn't eat.

To celebrate, he'd walked to Smyrna to visit his friend Rabbi Sarnoff and borrow a book. After tea and matzah, the senior rabbi of Chelm had taken his leave and his book, and begun reading as he walked home.

Now, Smyrna is a huge town, and with his nose in the book, Rabbi Kibbitz soon found himself lost. He looked up and saw he was in front of a shop, and figured he should go in and ask for directions.

He turned a page, opened the door, and was already at the counter before he realized that he'd made a huge mistake.

On the seventh day of Passover, Rabbi Kibbitz of Chelm found himself standing in the middle of a bakery full to the brim with fresh goods. It smelled sooo delicious.

He was about to turn and run when a large man stepped from the back room and introduced himself in a booming voice.

"Hiya! I'm Joe DaBaker! My name is my profession. I'm from America. I travel the world collecting recipes and sharing my knowledge. Everywhere I go, I open a shop for a few months, learn something new, and then move on. This is a beautiful town here, but it's strange, I haven't had a customer all week. What can I get you?"

Rabbi Kibbitz tried to be polite. He smiled. He was afraid that if he opened his mouth, he would begin to drool.

"Can I make a suggestion?" Joe said. "I have here a Brooklyn Chocolate Cake. It's seven layers of chocolate cake with a buttercream frosting, covered with a light chocolate ganache. I'll cut you a slice."

It was the most beautiful cake the wise man had ever seen.

"G-ummm," sputtered Rabbi Kibbitz.

"No cake?" the baker shrugged. "All right. What about this? I've got a blueberry pie with a chicken-shmaltz crust. That's something I learned here. Except instead of blueberries, since they're out of season, I have found a delicious sweet squash. I can cut you a slice..."

Rabbi Kibbitz stuttered, "Well, I, um..."

"How about an Italian Canolli?" the baker persisted. "It's basically sweet riccota cheese in a crisp tube. I learned the recipe in Florence. Or, if not that, I have a linzertorte from Vienna. It's sort of an Austrian shortbread filled with raspberry jam and sprinkled with powdered sugar. Or, I know! A Hungarian mocha layer cake with rum crème filling topped with a dollop of welfenpudding, which is a sweet vanilla custard thickened with cornstarch."

At the mention of each new delight, Rabbi Kibbitz thought a moment, and then shook his head fiercely.

"Strawberry chocolate croquembouche from Bordeaux, France? That's a cream puff pastry filled with chocolate and caramel and a little bit of red wine, drizzled with molten chocolate. Or a cinnamon *babka* recipe that learned here in Smyrna. It's absolutely heavenly."

"Wait!" Joe shouted. "I know. Toll House cookies from Whitman Massachussets. A butter cookie with huge chunks of chocolate chips. They're just about done. I can bring them to you warm from the oven. Maybe you'll eat them with a little milk?"

"G-ummm…. N'a… Er…" the rabbi groaned.

"Hmm," Joe said, scratching his head. "Maybe you don't like sweets? Not a problem. What about some bread?"

The rabbi felt weak and clutched the counter for support.

Joe persisted. He reached up on a shelf and brought down an enormous round flour-dusted loaf of bread, with a square pattern cut into the top of its crust.

"I call this Italian Paesano. I baked it from a sourdough I kept alive all the way from San Francisco. Take it home. Cut the slices thick. It's perfect for dipping after a dinner of pasta and gravy, which is a kind of a sauce."

Rabbi Kibbitz looked at the loaf, which was close enough to touch, but Joe didn't stop there. He grabbed a long skinny stick of bread, and began waving it in the rabbi's face.

"This is a Parisian French baguette! It's light with a crisp crust and snowy insides. Cut it lengthwise and serve it with cheese. Or, I also have this wonderful German Black Bread. Dark as night. Thick as a leg of lamb."

With that, he gestured toward a huge lump of what Rabbi Kibbitz at first took to be a small boulder. "I've heard that the Germans smear it with schmaltzy chicken fat, which to me is kindof disgusting."

Joe DaBaker shuddered.

Rabbi Kibbitz, however, couldn't help himself, and felt a dribble of drool seep out of his mouth and drip down his chin.

"Oh, you know what?" Joe said with a wide grin. "I just learned how to tie these things." He reached into a basket and pulled out a huge Bavarian pretzel. Big pieces of salt fell from it. "I think I have some spicy mustard somewhere under the counter."

"Gaaa!" Rabbi Kibbitz said. He felt as if his knees were buckling under him.

"What about a Polish rye bread? It's a dark and light swirl with lots of caraway seeds. I have some fresh-made butter that we can smear on it... Wait! I know. I finally figured it out."

Rabbi Kibbitz was startled by the sudden interruption. He stared at Joe, wondering what might possibly come next.

"Your Jewish!" Joe said, a glimmer of hope twinkling in his eye. "This is great. Just last week I got one of the bakers in Smyrna to show me how to make this."

He reached under the counter and lifted up a perfectly formed six-braided *challah.*

"This is an egg bread, right? You guys love these things for the holidays and Friday nights? This is the world's best *challah* recipe, and I've got three dozen of them sitting around. I can't understand why nobody's buying them."

"Ga.gaaa.gaaa.ggaaaaah!" Rabbi Kibbitz said, stumbling back. He barely had a hold of his book as he ran out of the shop.

"What did I say?" Joe muttered to himself. "Maybe he's got one of those newfangled wheat allergies. I dunno. It's so much easier in Manhattan. At least there, they know how to make bagels."

Rabbi Kibbitz ran all the way back to Chelm. By the time he arrived at his house, it was getting dark.

"You're late," his wife, said as he panted his way into the kitchen and collapsed at the table. She handed him a glass of water. "Are you hungry?"

He couldn't speak, but he nodded his head as he drank the water.

"What would you like?" she asked.

"What would I like to eat?" he replied softly.

"It's a simple question," she said.

"Me?" the rabbi said, his voice slowly rising to a fever pitch, "I'd like cake. I'd like pie. I'd like cookies. I'd like strudel. I want bread. I want rolls. I want pretzels. I want *challah* with shmaltz! Lots and lots and lots of it."

"It's still Passover," his wife said.

"I know," he said, rising to his feet, almost shouting. "I don't care. I want it all. I want it with butter and shmaltz. I want it dipped in gravy. I want it plain. I want it now!"

"All we have is matzah," she said.

The rabbi sighed. He collapsed in his chair. He shrugged. "All right. I'll have some matzah."

She set a piece on the table, and jumped back as he snatched it off the plate. "Be careful you don't eat my fingers," she said. "You want some chopped liver?"

His mouth full of dry tasteless crumbs, Rabbi Kibbitz nodded, closed his eyes, and dreamed of speed-reading his way through his book so he could return it to Smyrna in only two more days...

Home is Where the Seder Is

Abraham Schlemiel, his wife Rosa, and their son Abraham have moved to New York City, where they are about to celebrate their first Seder as a family…

Abraham Schlemiel stared into the empty soup bowl. He hoped that his feeling of dread wasn't showing on his face. What had he seen in *The Forward?* "Nobody can make chicken soup like a Jewish Mother." Rosa, his wife was good cook, but she was a gypsy. It wasn't the same. Still, she was trying.

The small table was set with most of the elements for the Passover Seder. On their best chipped plate lay a burned lamb bone, a pile of freshly grated horse radish, a porcelain thimble filled with salt water, a hard boiled egg, some slices of raw onion, and a mound of chopped lettuce. He'd given her a *Haggadah,* and she'd done her best. A stack of matzah lay on another plate beneath a beautiful red and purple scarf.

Abraham sneezed, barely getting his handkerchief up in time. He'd had this cold all winter.

"Bless you," Rosa said.

He looked up. Not two feet from where he sat, Rosa stood at the skinny stove, with her back to him, stirring the chicken soup. Because his nose was so stuffed, Abraham couldn't even smell the soup, which for the moment he decided might not be a bad thing.

Their apartment was so small. Little Abraham, their son, was dozing in the bathtub on the other side of the table. Not that he was so little any more. Abraham smiled at the boy, feeling badly that they couldn't afford a decent bed. Twelve years old. Every morning he was up at dawn selling newspapers to the bankers on Wall Street. Then he went to school, and after that there were the preparations for his *bar mitzvah*, plus the violin practice that his mother insisted on.

Abraham had offered to cook. He worked as a chef at Fraunces Tavern*, the oldest restaurant in New York, on Pearl Street near the tip of Manhattan. It was ironic, a Jew working in a treif establishment, but he managed by bringing his own lunch and asking his helpers to taste the food for him. The joke was that Abraham's dishwashers ate better than he did.

"No, I'll cook," Rosa had said. "Your Passover is a day for tradition. The tradition is that the wife cooks, and the husband leads the, what do you call it, Saber?"

"Seder," he corrected. "After a long day of sewing hems, you want to do everything yourself? I'd be happy to help."

"You cook all day," she said, firmly. "Besides there's not so much to do."

Abraham blinked as he remembered his mother and grandmother and his baby sister, Shmeini, scurrying around the kitchen for weeks in preparation.

He missed home. He missed Chelm in the springtime with its muddy streets and the sharp scent of spring in the air. New York wasn't paved with gold. You found that out pretty quickly after you arrived. The cobblestone streets were filled with holes, and the sidewalks were filthy from horses and dogs. At least in Chelm the worst you would do is fill your boot with mud. He missed the shul, and the rabbis, the constant gossip and discussions in Yiddish, Russian and Polish. The languages on Orchard Street were familiar, but the work was so different. In New York there were no farmers. And everything was so crowded.

Most of all he missed his family. His father, mother, sister and of course Adam. They were twins. How could they not miss each other? For a moment, Abraham tried reaching out in his mind, trying to send his thoughts across the ocean and a continent to his brother. But Adam was either asleep or not listening. Nothing.

"It's time," Rosa said.

In his bathtub, young Abraham yawned and stretched. Rosa passed out the *Haggadahs* and lit the candles. She helped her husband wash his hands. She listened carefully as he told her, for the first time, the story of the Exodus from Egypt.

They both beamed as their son read the four questions perfectly.

As Abraham sped through the service, he remembered the battles that he and Adam had fought over who was the youngest, who would have the honor of reading the questions. He missed his grandparents, who always made jokes and helped with the singing by humming so badly off key that anyone's voice sounded good.

At last it was time for dinner, the moment Abraham had been dreading.

She brought the heavy soup pot to the table, which shuddered under its weight.

"Before you eat," she said, sitting down. "I have to apologize. This is all we have. I wanted to make the *kiggel* and *kugel* and *giggle*, or whatever else you call what you're used to eating. I was going to roast a brisket. But there was a fire at another factory, and the girls' families needed some money to help with the hospital bills. I gave away what we had, and kept just enough for the soup."

"You did well." Abraham smiled, resting his hand gently on hers. Amazing how much he loved her after all these years.

Their son tried hard not to look disappointed.

"Don't worry," she said, "We've got plenty of matzah balls, and I saved some chicken from the soup so that it wouldn't taste like rubber."

Rosa lifted the lid of her grandmother's pot, and ladled out portions into each of their bowls.

Abraham hoped for the best. Whether it was too salty or too weak or too vinegary or too peppery, he promised himself he would say nothing. If the matzah balls were rock hard, crumbly dry, or raw in the middle, he would keep his mouth shut. His face would remain neutral, and then he would feign joy and delight.

His spoon dipped down into the rich golden broth. He brought it to his lips, and slurped.

In an instant, his nose cleared and for the first time in weeks he could smell. He smelled the soup! The rich aroma filled his nose, the warm taste filled his mouth, and his face broke into a grin. The miracle of chicken soup!

He nodded, and then steeled himself as he stared at the matzah balls.

Tentatively he cut into a knaidel, and it broke cleanly. He raised it to his lips and chewed. Not that he had to chew very much. Firm, yet light, it was filled with a hearty flavor that was indescribable.

"Well?" Rosa said, waiting for the verdict.

"It is home," Abraham said simply. He reached over and took his wife's hand. "We need nothing more than each other, but if we are allowed only one other thing, I certainly hope it is this soup."

Rosa glowed. Young Abraham laughed with his father.

And the small family lived happily in their cramped apartment, until they moved to the suburbs. But that, as they say, is another story.

**Fraunces Tavern is the oldest-still operating restaurant in New York City. Built in 1762, it is most famous for the farewell banquet that George Washington gave for his officers in 1783 after the revolutionary war.*

Chelm Will Not Go Hungry

Two weeks before Pesach, Rabbi Yohon Abrahms and his Yeshiva students were discussing Passover preparations. A lively debate had arisen over the definition of leavened bread…

"I still don't see why we can't use yeast," said Joel Cantor. "In Exodus it just says that the bread didn't have time to rise."

"They didn't know about yeast in those days," said Jacob Stein, the baker's son, who knew the complete history of bread. "They just left the bread out and waited for it to rise, because the yeast was floating in the air."

Rabbi Abrahms was pleased at his student's enthusiasm. He tugged on his beard, and said, "Tell me, David, what do you think?"

David Gold, the son of the cobbler, did not hesitate. He stood up and fled from the room.

"What did I say?" Rabbi Abrahms asked the rest of his students.

Joel Cantor raised his hand. "The Golds are not eating matzah this year."

Rabbi Abrahms was shocked, "What? Why?"

Martin Levitsky said, "It's too expensive."

"It is not!" Jacob Stein said, defending his father's bakery, which was known for its delicious matzah.

"They still can't afford it," said a quiet voice. It was Rachel Cohen, the daughter of the tailor, the first girl who had ever been admitted to the Yeshiva.

"Hmm," Rabbi Abrahms stroked his beard

thoughtfully. "Perhaps we should discuss *tsedaka*, charity..."

Later that evening, the Village Council of Elders summoned Reb Gold to the Synagogue's meeting hall. Behind the long table sat Rabbi Kibbitz, Reb Cantor the Merchant and Reb Stein the Baker.

Reb Gold stood before them with his hat held in his hand, and his head bare except for his kippah.

"Joshua," Rabbi Kibbitz began, "we are sorry to bring you here like this."

"What do you mean, you're not going to buy my matzah!" snapped Reb Stein.

"Shh," Rabbi Kibbitz raised his hand. "This is an inquiry, not an inquisition."

Reb Gold looked at the floor and spoke in a quiet voice, "We have no money."

"Then I'll give you the matzah," barked Reb Stein. "When you get some money, you'll give me what you can."

"No one buys shoes from me any more," Reb Gold said plainly. "Not since the shoe factory in Smyrna was built. Shoes from there cost less than my materials alone."

The elders shifted uncomfortably, for every one of them was wearing a pair of shoes from that factory.

"You can still repair shoes, can't you?" asked Reb Cantor.

"Why? Are your shoes worn out?" replied Reb Gold.

"Not yet," Reb Cantor admitted.

Reb Gold shrugged. "I would never be able to repay Reb Stein for the matzah. We have a large bag of rice in the cellar. My family will eat that until after Passover."

"Rice!" bellowed Reb Stein, "Nonsense! You will eat my matzah!"

"Quiet! " Rabbi Kibbitz commanded. Reb Stein fell silent. "It is common," the rabbi continued, "for the town of Chelm to take care of its citizens."

"I cannot accept charity forever," Reb Gold said.

"Then what will you do," asked Reb Cantor, "when you run out of rice?"

Reb Gold looked down at his shoes. They were well made shoes, beautifully crafted. His father had taught him how to make shoes, like his grandfather and great grandfather. Perhaps they were not as stylish as those from the factory, but they would last for years—for decades. He had gone so far as to visit the factory in Smyrna to ask for a job, even though it was a three hour walk in each direction. The factory owner had shown him how the shoes were made. Each man in the factory worked on just one part of the shoe—the sole, the heel, the cuff, the tongue. The owner offered Reb Gold the job of punching eyelets. That would be it, day in and day out—punching eyelets—not even threading laces! Reb Gold was a craftsman, not a machine. He had graciously refused the job, and walked sadly back to Chelm.

"Have you any family?" asked Rabbi Kibbitz.

"Does he have family?" Reb Stein laughed, "They visit all the time! From all over Russia and Poland. Even from as far away as England. They come into my shop and marvel at the *challah*."

"They come into my store," agreed Reb Cantor, "and they always buy something for souvenirs."

"I will not become a beggar and impose on my family!" cried Reb Gold, who was nearly in tears. "I will not take my family away and leave my home. Chelm is the most beautiful place in the world! Our streets are well kept, our round square is beautiful. The trees bloom with pink flowers in the spring and then the leaves turn brilliant in autumn. The water is pure, and the mind of every person who lives here is bright with wonder and astonishment.

"If I leave Chelm, I know what everyone will say. 'Look, there goes Joshua Gold. He was too stupid to stay in Chelm!'"

The poor cobbler fell silent, and rather than look at his shoes, he closed his eyes.

Reb Cantor, on the other hand, was smiling. "I have an idea!"

"What's a travel agent?" Esther Gold asked her husband when he returned home that evening.

"I will bring visitors to Chelm!" Joshua Gold answered with excitement. "I will organize tours. People will come from far and wide to our little village, and when they go they will take lots of souvenirs and presents, and a little bit of the wisdom of Chelm home with them."

"Does it pay?" Esther asked, not daring to hope.

"Enough. I'll also make shoes," Joshua answered, patting his wife's hand. "To begin I will work for Reb Cantor. When the tourists arrive, I will receive a commission."

"All this for talking and getting people to come and visit?" She rolled her eyes. "What will they think of next?"

"Maybe we could open a hotel?" suggested young David Gold.

Reb Gold smiled at his son. "Thank you, David, for sharing our burden. Without you, and the help of the others, this would have been a very difficult year."

With that, the small family gathered together, and hugged each other with joy.

Was Reb Gold successful? Of course! That, my friends, is why the story of the small village of Chelm is told far and wide, even to the ends of the planet.

A Chelm Dictionary

"A word clearly spoken is like a pattern of golden apples on a silver mosaic."
—Proverbs 25: 11

Yiddish is a language of sound and subtlety. Hebrew is an ancient tongue. This is a Chelmenish interpretation of words you may, or may not know.

Chelm: the village where most of the people in this book live. A traditional source of Jewish humor. The "ch" in Chelm (and most Yiddish and Hebrew transliteration) is pronounced like you've got something stuck in your throat. "Ch-elm."

Chelmener: the people who live in Chelm. Often known as the wisefolk of Chelm. Sometimes called Chelmites. Sometimes called, "The Fools of Chelm".

babka: a delicious cake. Usually served with coffee, tea and gossip.

Bar Mitzvah: the Jewish coming-of-age ceremony. Celebrated at 13. The day most boys become fountain pens. Almost always catered.

bimah: the platform at the front of the synagogue where the rabbi stands so that everyone can hear him.

Cantor: a person who leads a religious service with song. Not to be confused with Reb Cantor the merchant.

challah: a braided egg bread. In English, the plural of challah is challah. (If we may recommend… after Passover get a copy of Mark's book, "*The World's Best Challah*" and make your own!)

Chanukah: the festival of lights. Celebrated in the winter, it commemorates the victory of the Maccabees over the Syrians. The miracle of Chanukah was that one day's measure of oil burned in the Temple for eight days. Sometimes spelled Hanukkah. Or Hanukah.

chometz: all sorts of delicious baked goods that aren't matzah. Only obsessed about during Passover.

dreidel: a four-sided top spun in a children's game during Chanukah. Although sometimes played for money, Dreidel is usually played for high stakes, like raisins and nuts.

erev: the evening that begins a holiday. Jewish holidays start at sunset and end after sunset.

goyishe: something that is not Jewish.

goob: when something is so delicious that you can't pronounce the letter "d" because you're too busy eating, it's "goob."

hamotzi: blessing over the bread—or matzah.

kabalah: Jewish mysticism, often numerological. It's secret: shhh!

kiggel (or kugel): a pudding. Mmmm.

knaidel: a matzah ball dumpling served in chicken soup. Often served during Passover. The plural of knaidel is knaidlach.

kreplach: a dumpling. Jewish wontons. Tasty!

kvell: to glow with pride.

latke: a pancake fried in oil. At Passover, latkes are made with matzah meal. At Hanukkah they are made with potatoes.

mishugas: craziness.

mitzvah: a commandment, often a good deed. Not to be confused with a Bar Mitzvah, which is the coming of age ceremony for boys.

mashgiach - the rabbi in charge of making sure everything's kosher.

mensch: a good guy. A nice fellah. Kind and generous. You want your daughter to marry one.

matzah: unleavened bread made from flour and water with no salt or yeast. Sometimes spelled "matzoh." Eaten during Passover, the holiday celebrating the Exodus from Egypt. Also known as the bread of affliction, perhaps because it is tasteless, bland and binding.

matzah brie: fried matzah. Mix damp matzah with eggs and salt and fry it to make matzah brie. Yum!

oy: an expression of excitement and often pain. "Oy! My back." or "Oy, I can't believe you're wearing that to a wedding!"

Passover/Pesach: the celebration of the Exodus from Egypt. Celebrated for eight days in the diaspora or seven day, depending on where you live and what you believe.

plotz: to explode. As in, "I ate so much matzah brie I nearly plotzed."

Rabbi: a scholar, a teacher, a leader in the community.

Reb: a wise man. And, since everyone in Chelm is wise, the men are all called Reb… as in Reb Stein, Reb Cantor and so on.

Seder: the Passover feast. A huge meal with lots of prayers, songs and stories. No leavened bread. No challah. Just matzah. Followed by seemingly endless days of matzah. Oy.

Shabbas: the Jewish Sabbath. Starts Friday at sundown and ends Saturday after sunset. Sometimes called Shabbat or Shabbos.

shmear: a big hunk of cream cheese usually spread on a bagel, but during Passover you can shmear matzah.

Shmura Matzah: a special round matzah made from carefully guarded wheat. Often burned. Don't use it for matzah brie.

Smyrna: the nearest town to Chelm.

shmaltz: chicken fat. Used in cooking and spread on bread. Source of many heart attacks.

shmootz: dust, dirt, those little brown flecks of stuff that you find here and there.

Shul: the synagogue.

Torah: the five books of Moses. The first five books of the Bible.

tsedaka: a gift of charity.

tuchas: the posterior.

yad: a pointer. You're not supposed to touch the Torah Scroll as you read, so instead of pointing with your finger, you use a yad. The word means hand, so it often looks just like a tiny hand with its index finger outstretched.

Yom Kippur: the day of atonement. No one eats or drinks. No kiggle, knaidel, babke, challah or shmaltz or even matzah. Always followed by the break-fast, a sumptuous meal served after dark. All the food is eaten in a matter of moments.

yenta: a gossip, a busybody.

yeshiva: the religious school. In Chelm, the yeshiva is the only school.

zaftig: plump, but in a good way. Rubenesque.

Preparing Family Stories—a recipe

What stories don't we tell our children? Passover is a time for telling stories, but we often neglect the stories that are closest to our hearts.

A number of years ago, I had the good fortune to interview both of my father's parents. I recorded the conversations and later on we had them transcribed. I learned more about my grandparents in two hours than I had in the decades before that.

A few years after that, I performed a similar interview with my mother and father, and I learned to love my parents on a different level.

Do you tell you children how you were married? Or when you first met your partner? Do you tell them how you got interested in your job? Or what your home was like when you were a youngster?

Chances are you don't. Chances are, your parents didn't tell you much and you're likely to pass along this unfortunate habit to your children.

There are plenty of reasons that we don't share our own personal stories. Business, laziness and embarrassment are high up on the list of excuses. There are also plenty of reasons that we don't know our family's stories. (See above, and add in fear of upsetting someone.)

There is, however, a simple solution.

Start telling the stories of your life. Start asking your parents and grandparents to share their stories.

But wait, you say, that's impossible. How do you even begin?

Let's start with the premise that your loved ones are still alive. If they are, then you can talk with them. (If they're not, you can take these steps and use them to ask anyone who knew them about your relatives. You'll be surprised how much you can learn.)

Plan time at your Seder to gather these stories. Even if you don't go hi-tech, there are plenty of opportunities between cooking and cleaning and eating to talk and listen. Remember to listen…

Thirteen Steps for Interviewing Your Family

1. Buy or borrow a digital recording device. You can find these online, at electronics stores and office supply stores. (If you're really cheap or broke, you can always return the device to the stores after you've used it…) Don't worry too much about recording quality. Make sure you have enough memory to record for at least an hour, preferably two. Practice with this device. Make sure you know how it works before you run your interview. Test it out. Figure out how to get the recording off the device.
2. Schedule the time and date with your family members. Be sure that you'll have at

least two hours together. Even if you don't use the whole time, it's good to have the space. DON'T interview just one parent and not the other. You don't have to do a marathon, but make sure they all know that they're all going to have their say.

3. Make a list of questions. Make a huge and long list, but don't get attached to it. In other words, you won't get to ask every question on your list. The objective is to hear stories, and stories don't necessarily answer questions, but they can be inspired by them.

   Some categories of questions include

   a. Where did you grow up? What did your parents do?
   b. What kinds of food did you eat?
   c. Do you remember any smells from when you were a child? (Smell is a powerful memory activator)
   d. How did you meet Mom/Dad?
   e. Did you ever fight in a war? What was that like? (Be cautious with this one.)
   f. What was the hardest time of your life?
   g. What was the easiest time of your life
4. Ask your children to contribute questions to the list

5. Remind everyone in advance that you're going to do the interview. If they try to back out, reschedule
6. On the day of the interview make sure that the house is neat, the chores are done and put on a pot of tea or coffee. Have water and snacks available.
7. Test your recording device again in the location you are doing the interviews. Make sure you have extra batteries or it's plugged in. Make sure it's recording. Listen to it. (You *will* want to kill yourself if you blow this by not checking the electronics…)
8. Let the recording device run. Don't look at it. Just ignore it and write notes on your paper. After about 10 minutes it will become invisible. Look in their eyes, not at the recorder. The longer it runs, the better it gets.
9. Ask your questions, but listen for stories. Follow the threads of the conversation rather than sticking with your list.
10. Don't get discouraged if they get stuck. Ask about other people in their lives. Ask about details. Listen to the silence. Ask how they felt.

11. When you have finished, be sure to press stop on the recorder. Digital devices may erase if you let their batteries die before pressing stop. Later on you can make copies for your relatives and share it with your children.
12. Thank them and give them a hug. No matter what you got on the audio recording, the time you spent with your family was worth it.
13. Be sure to tell and retell these stories, and add them to the stories you tell your children and grandchildren.

About the Author

Mark Binder is an award-winning author and storyteller.

He has been writing for adults and children for more than two decades.

Hundreds of his stories for young and old have been published in magazines, anthologized in books, and used on standardized tests.

Mark's books and audio recordings have won numerous awards. His educational performances in school and library settings draw raves from students, faculty, administrators and parents. In addition to a vast repertoire of entertaining and educational stories, he has the unique ability to read a room and instantly adjust the program based on the age range of the audience present. His workshops are transformative. He transmits joy through language and story.

He is the founder of the American Story Theater, and has taught a college course in "Telling Lies" at the Rhode Island School of Design. He holds a third degree black belt and teaches and practices centering and Aikido, the martial art for peace. In his spare time he bakes bread and makes pizza.

Mark lives in Providence, RI with his three children.

Please look for Mark Binder's other works

BOOKS

It Ate My Sister

The Brothers Schlemiel

The Bed Time Story Book

A Hanukkah Present

The Council of Wise Women

The Rationalization Diet

AUDIO

Adventures with Giants and Slugs

Classic Stories for Boys and Girls

Tall Tales, Whoppers and Lies

Dead at Knotty Oak

A Chanukkah Present

The Brothers Schlemiel From Birth to Bar Mitzvah

These fine books and audio recordings are available by ordering directly from your local bookstore or favorite online provider, including Amazon.Com, the Kindle, CDBaby.com, and the iTunes music store.

Have an excellent day!

For a free story, as well as the most recent books, audio, weblog and stories by Mark Binder *plus* information about his touring schedule and entertaining and educational programs please visit www.markbinder.com

Printed in the United States
221981BV00001B/5/P

9 780982 470718